On Market Street

On Market Street

Pictures by
Anita Lobel

Words by Arnold Lobel

Scholastic Inc.
New York Toronto London Auckland Sydney

ISBN 0-590-41004-0

12 11 10 9 8 7 6 5 4   9/8 0/9

Printed in the U.S.A   08

To Timothy and Susan Benn

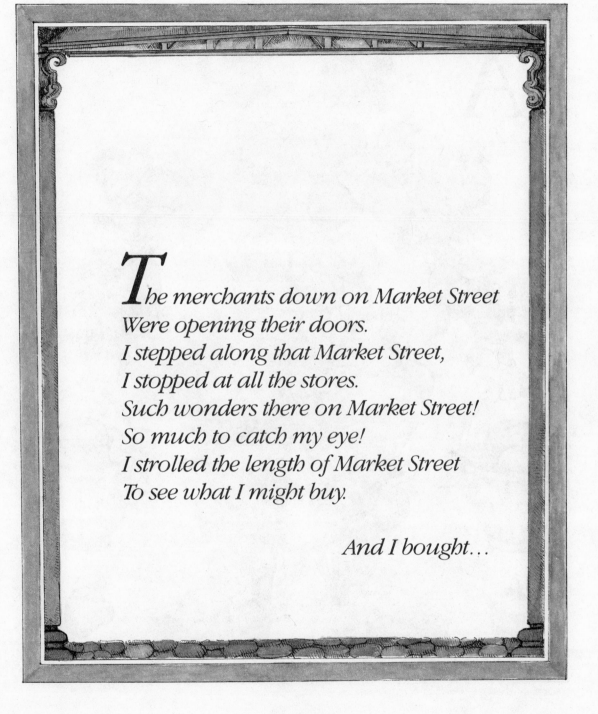

The merchants down on Market Street
Were opening their doors.
I stepped along that Market Street,
I stopped at all the stores.
Such wonders there on Market Street!
So much to catch my eye!
I strolled the length of Market Street
To see what I might buy.

And I bought…

apples,

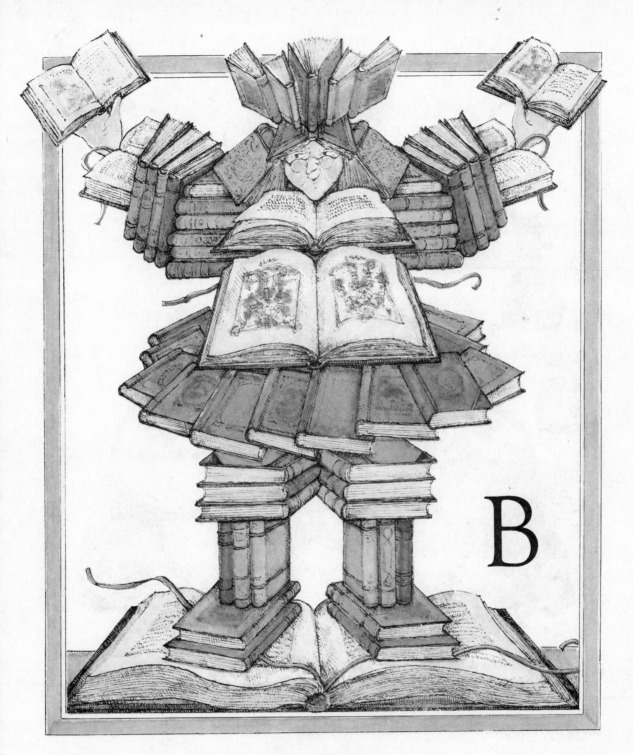

books,

clocks,

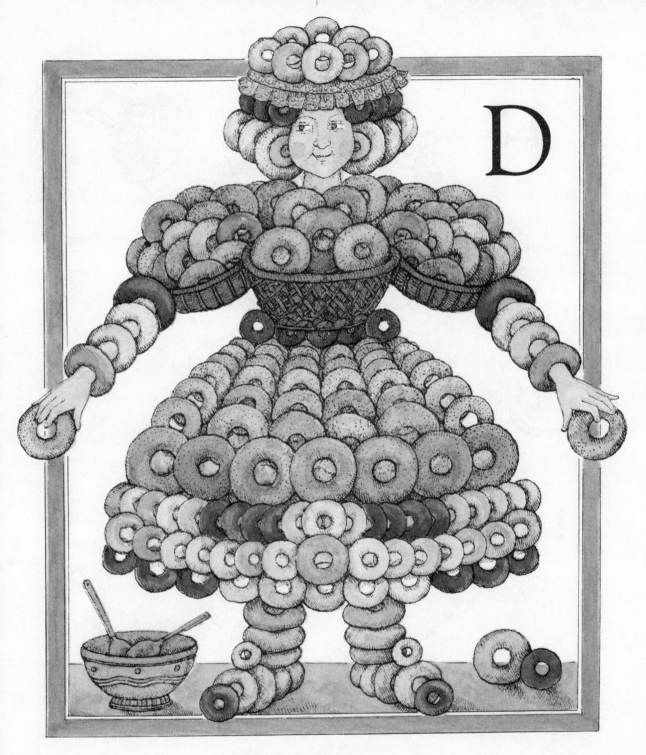

doughnuts,

eggs,

F

flowers,

gloves,

hats,

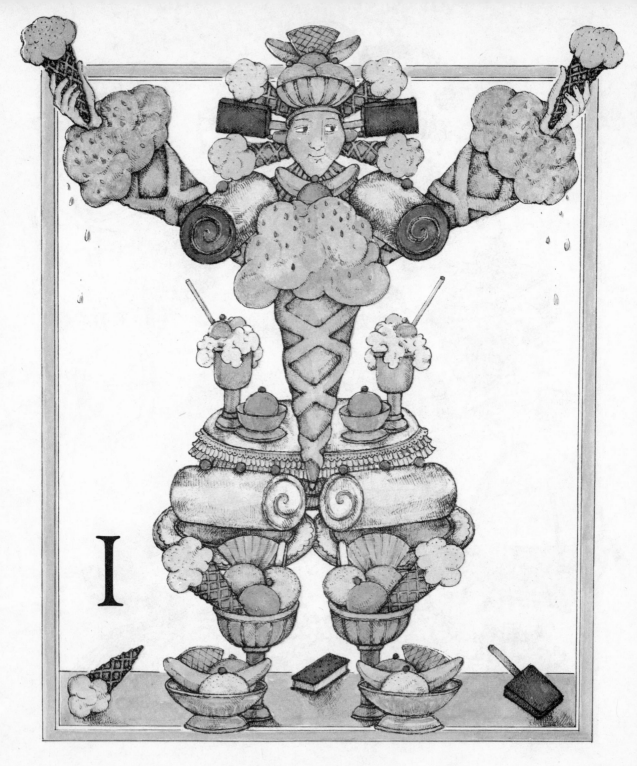

I

ice cream,

jewels,

K

kites,

lollipops,

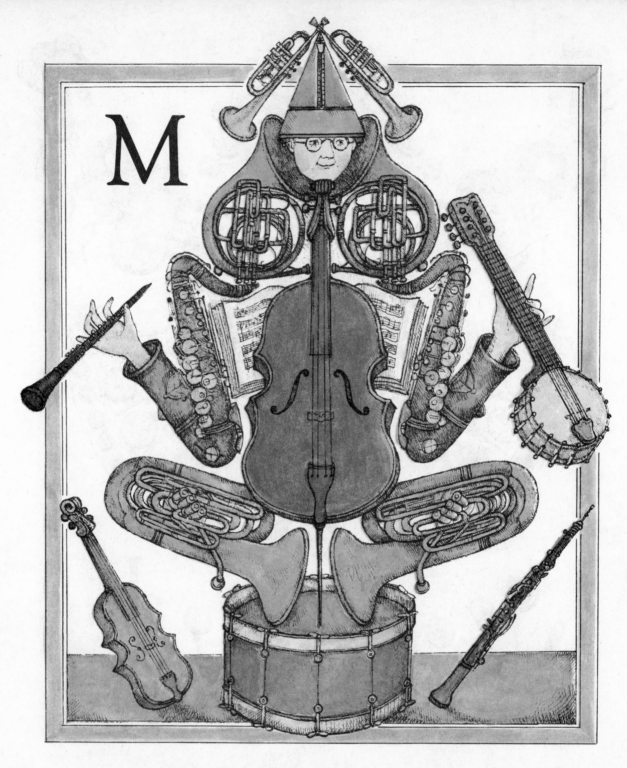

M

musical instruments,

noodles,

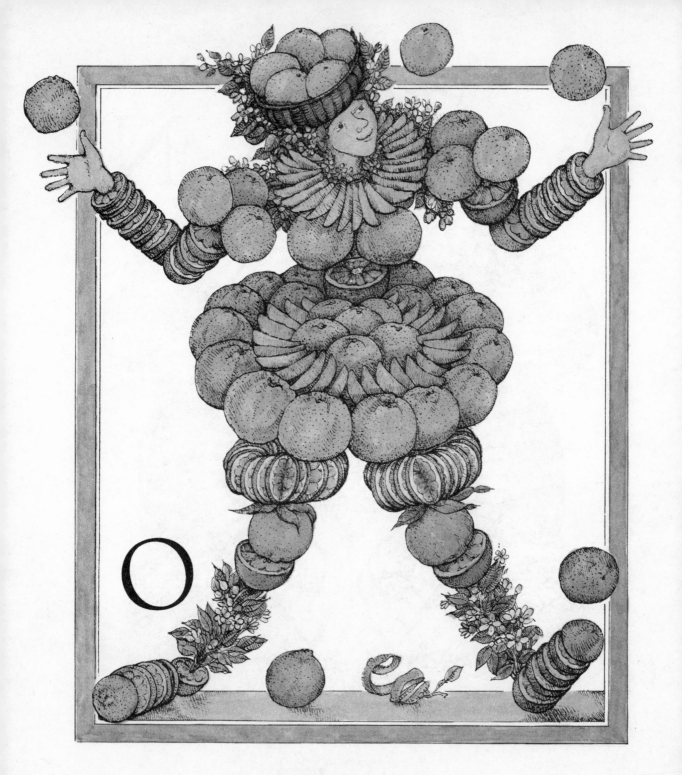

oranges,

P

playing cards,

quilts,

ribbons,

shoes,

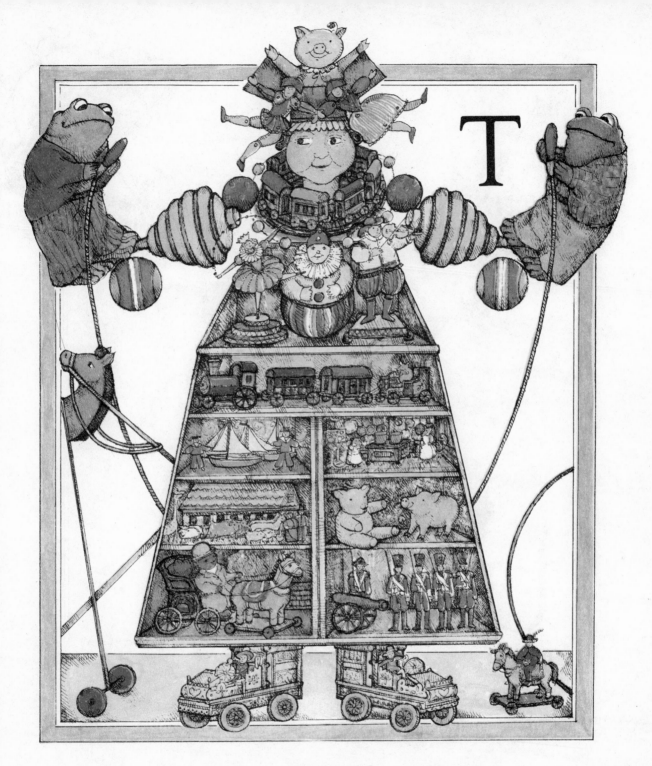

toys,

umbrellas,

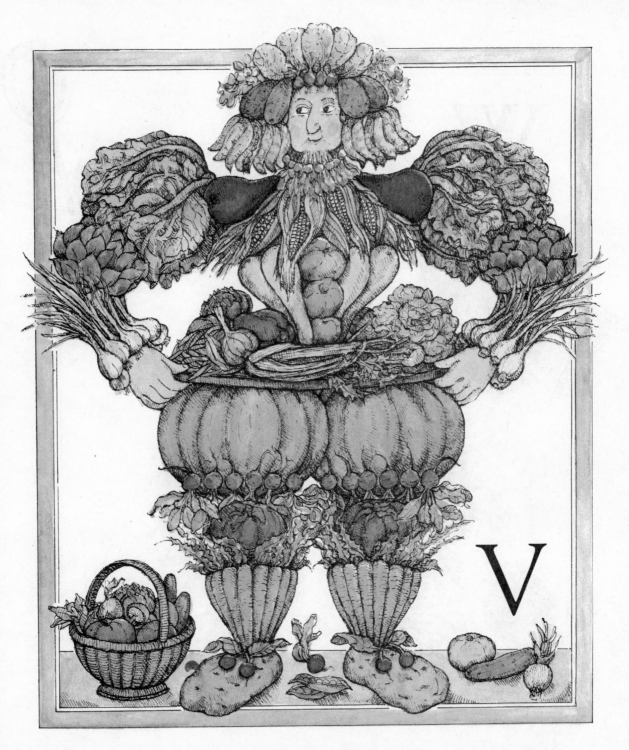

vegetables,

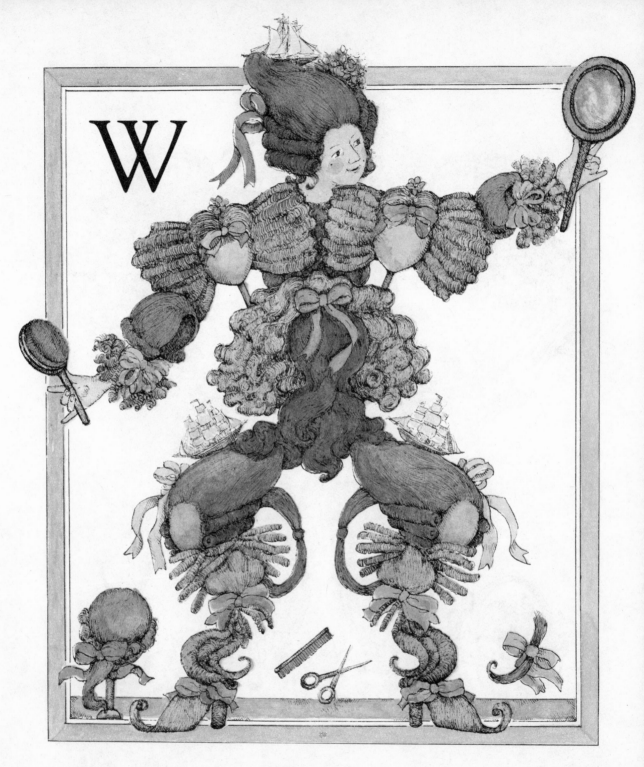

wigs,

Xmas trees,

yarns,

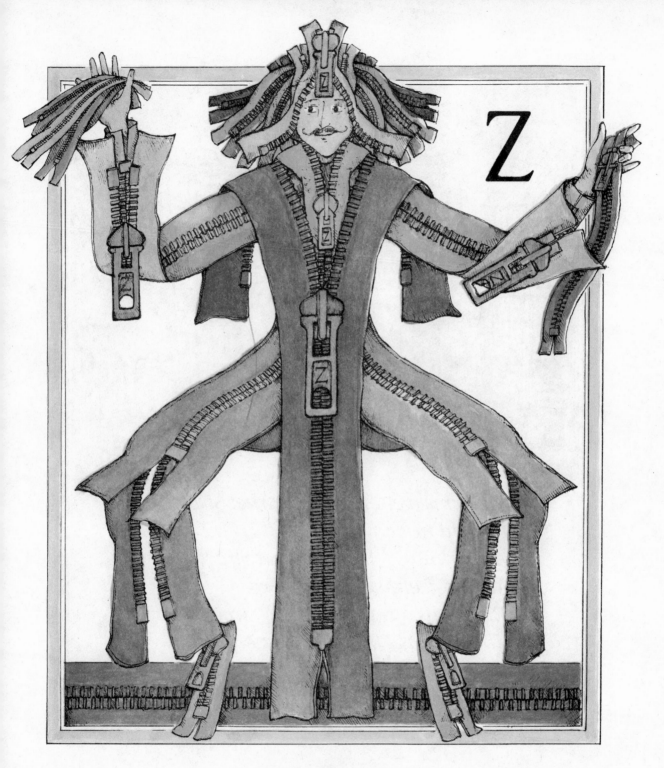

zippers.

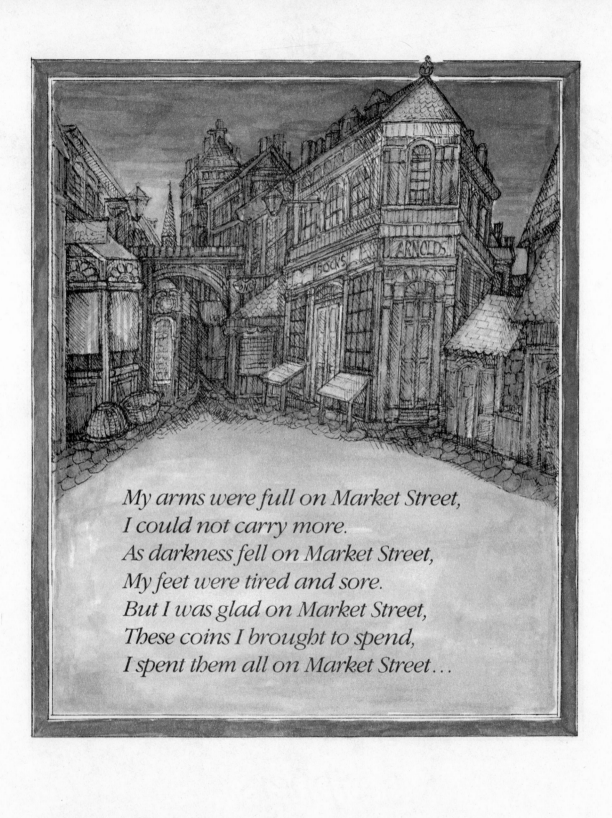

My arms were full on Market Street,
I could not carry more.
As darkness fell on Market Street,
My feet were tired and sore.
But I was glad on Market Street,
These coins I brought to spend,
I spent them all on Market Street…

…on presents for a friend.

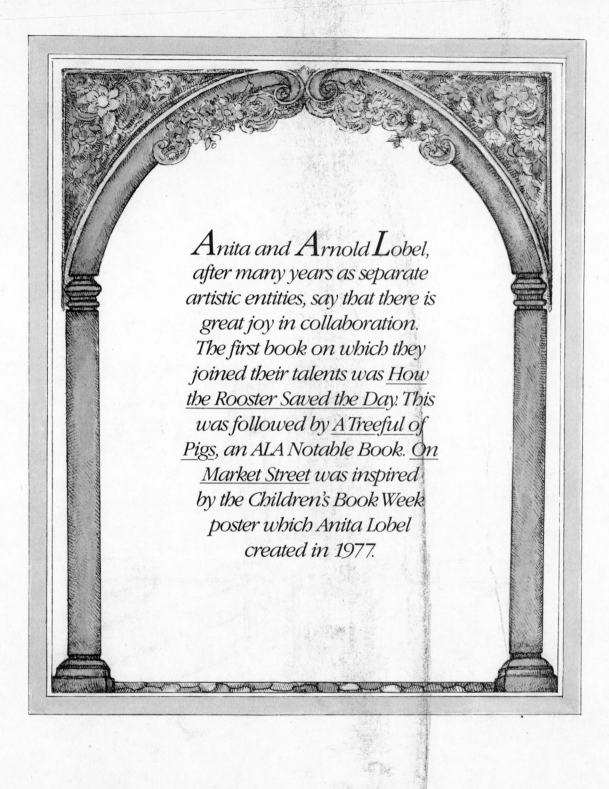

Anita and Arnold Lobel, after many years as separate artistic entities, say that there is great joy in collaboration. The first book on which they joined their talents was How the Rooster Saved the Day. *This was followed by* A Treeful of Pigs, *an ALA Notable Book.* On Market Street *was inspired by the Children's Book Week poster which Anita Lobel created in 1977.*